Scholastic Publications Ltd.,
10 Earlham Street, London WC2H 9RX, UK

Scholastic Inc.,
730 Broadway, New York, NY 10003, USA

Scholastic Tab Publications Ltd.,
123 Newkirk Road, Richmond Hill,
Ontario L4C 3G5, Canada

Ashton Scholastic Pty. Ltd.,
P O Box 579, Gosford, New South Wales,
Australia

Ashton Scholastic Ltd.,
165 Marua Road, Panmure, Auckland 6,
New Zealand

First published by Scholastic Publications Limited, 1989
Text copyright © John Cunliffe, 1989
Illustrations copyright © Scholastic Publications Limited and
Woodland Animations Limited, 1989

ISBN 0 590 85853 X

Made and printed in Hong Kong
Typeset in Times Roman by AKM Associates (UK) Ltd,
Ajmal House, Hayes Road, Southall, London

Postman Pat's
Market Day

Story by **John Cunliffe** *Pictures by* **Joan Hickson**
From the original Television designs by **Ivor Wood**

Hippo Books
in association with André Deutsch

Pat was looking through the *Pencaster Gazette*. On the back page there was a big advertisement that said,

---

PENCASTER AUCTION MARKET
LIMITED
ANNUAL PRIZE SHOW AND
SALE – SATURDAY
20th SEPTEMBER
AT 10.30 a.m.
All classes of sheep, cattle and poultry.
Goats and pigs.

"Look at that," said Pat. "It's years and years since I went to market. I do love a good sale. And it's a show as well."

"Why don't you go?" said Mrs Goggins, looking over his shoulder.

"It starts at 10.30," said Pat. "I'll be busy with my letters."

"It'll go on all day, with all that to sell. You'll not miss much," said Mrs Goggins. "I've seen Herbert Pottage coming back from a big sale at six and seven o'clock."

"I bet young Julian would like it," said Pat. "He's never been to market."

That Saturday, the letters were sorted
and delivered in record time. Pat, and
Sara, and Julian, caught the Greendale
bus at half-past twelve. Miss Hubbard
was driving, and she had four large
baskets on the luggage-rack, with lids on
them.

Pat puzzled about those baskets all the way to Pencaster. They looked like cat-baskets, but Pat knew that Miss Hubbard didn't have any cats, let alone four. He meant to ask her, but the bus was soon full and she was too busy for conversation.

When they got to Pencaster, they had beans on toast at Mosscrop's cafe. Then Pat said, "We'll be off to the market, then."

"I haven't time for the market," said Sara. "Somebody has to do the shopping, you know."

"We'd better come and help," said Pat.

"No, it's all right," said Sara. "There isn't all that much shopping, and I want to pick a new pair of shoes in peace. I can manage. We'll meet for a cup of tea at four, in time for the five o'clock bus."

It was a long walk to the market. It was on the edge of the town, where there was plenty of room for all the trucks and trailers that brought the cows, and sheep, and goats, and pigs in to the market. There was a big car-park, too, and it was filled with the farmers' cars and Land-Rovers, and vans, and tractors, and horse-boxes. There were pens for the animals waiting to be sold, and there was a field at the back, full of noisy bullocks.

Even though the sale had been on for almost three hours, new waggons full of sheep and cattle were still driving up. Others were loading up with animals that had been sold. There was bleating and mooing, and the grunting and squealing of pigs. There was the shouting of farmers and their men as they drove the cattle into the pens. And the market had its special mixture of smells; animals, and petrol, and concrete-floors washed with disinfectant.

"What a pong!" said Julian.
"And what a noise!" said Pat. "I'd forgotten what it's like."

There were crowds of farmers and their wives inside and outside. Some were looking at the lists of animals for sale. Some were going round the pens having a good look at a sow or a goat they might fancy. Some were shaking hands on a deal. Some were counting out rolls of ten-pound notes.

Some were just having a good chat with friends and relations.

Pat and Julian had to push and squeeze their way in, past all this busy-ness. At last, they found a corner where they could see all that was going on inside the market.

There was a space in the middle, a bit like a circus-ring, where the animals were brought to be sold. There were passages and gates leading into it. All round the ring were galleries where the people stood. Above the ring, there was a special box that made Julian think of the pulpit in church where the Reverend Timms stood on Sundays.

But the Reverend was not in it. Instead there was the most important man at the market; the auctioneer. He stood up there, at a little desk, with a wooden hammer in his hand, and looked down on everybody.

He announced each animal as it came into the ring, in a voice that rang round that noisy place so clear and loud that everyone heard him. He said who was selling it, how heavy it was, and how old it was. Then he banged his hammer on the desk, looked around at everyone, and said, "Come along now, ladies and gentlemen, who'll start us off?

What am I bid? Shall I say a hundred-and-sixty? Who'll give me a hundred-and-sixty? One-sixty? Thank you, Sir! One-sixty? Seventy? Eighty – eighty – eighty-five, eighty-five, eighty-five; who'll say ninety? One hundred-and-ninety pounds for this fine sow? Ninety? Thank you, madam. Ninety-five, ninety-five . . . two hundred . . . yes? Thank you! Two hundred? Two hundred? Any more bids? Two hundred? Will anyone say two hundred and ten? No? Two hundred? Is that your best bid, ladies and gentlemen? Going at two hundred to the lady over there! Going for the first time!" (Bang with the hammer.) "Going for the second time!" (Bang with the hammer.) "Going for the third time!" (A final bang with the hammer, and a word in his ear from one of the helpers.) "Sold to Mrs Cowan at two hundred pounds. And next . . ." and off he was again.

Julian was in a muddle. How did he
know that Mrs Cowan wanted that pig?
She hadn't said anything at all.

All she had done was to nod and smile.
Julian thought it was a funny way to
spend two hundred pounds. Some people
seemed to give the auctioneer a little wave
when they wanted to buy something, or
just touched their cap or hat. The
auctioneer seemed to muddle the
numbers up, too. He went faster and
faster. Sometimes, when a lot of people
wanted something, he got into a high-
speed gabble, and Julian couldn't tell a
word he said.

"Look," said Pat. "There's Miss Hubbard in her new hat. She's come to the market between bus-trips. Give her a wave. Hello, Miss Hubbard!" Pat waved, and the auctioneer said, "Thank you, Sir, one-fifty, and . . . two hundred over there . . ." But Pat was so busy admiring Miss Hubbard's hat that he didn't seem to notice what the auctioneer was saying.

"Dad," said Julian, "I think . . ." But the auctioneer was off again, and Pat couldn't hear Julian.

Then Pat spotted Mr and Mrs Pottage
and the twins.
"Hello!" he called, waving and smiling
across at them.

"Sixty-five," said the auctioneer. "And seventy to the lady over there."

"Dad . . ." said Julian.

But Pat had seen Alf Thompson.

"He must have come to buy some lambs," said Pat. "Alf! Hello, there!" And he waved to Alf.

"Fifty," said the auctioneer, "and a bargain at the price. Any more bids? Going, going, going, gone, at fifty pounds, to the gentleman with the blue scarf."

"That's you dad," said Julian.

"What?" said Pat.

"You've bought a goat. You're the man in the blue scarf."

"A goat?" said Pat. "I haven't! I haven't bought anything."

"You were waving at Alf, and that auctioneer-man thought you were waving to say you wanted to buy that goat."

"A goat?" said Pat. "Oh, dear, how much was it?"

"Fifty pounds," said Julian. "That's what he said."

"Oh dear," said Pat. "What a muddle. Whatever shall we do?"

"It's a very nice goat," said Julian.

"It might well be a very nice goat, but what are we going to do with a goat?" said Pat.

"We could milk it," said Julian. "I love goat's milk, and so does mum."

"Does she?" said Pat.

"Yes," said Julian, "and it would keep the grass short in the garden. It'd save you having to cut it."

"It'll keep the flowers short as well," said Pat.

By now, the auctioneer's helpers had come to take Pat's address. And one of them was saying, "Could you collect by 6 pm Sir? Pen number twenty-three."

"Er . . . yes," said Pat.

"And take this slip to the office, with your payment."

"Thank you," said Pat.

So this is how Pat and Julian came to be walking through the middle of Pencaster on Saturday afternoon, with a very lively goat, using a length of binder-twine as a lead. A frisky goat in an empty field is bad enough. In the middle of Pencaster it was something that Pat would never ever forget! He never knew how they managed to get to the tea-shop where they were meeting Sara.

The goat was surprisingly strong. It
pulled Pat this way and that way, any
way except the way he wanted to go. It
tried to butt people. It went nosing under
market-stalls to nibble at dropped
vegetables and fruit. It tried to get into a
supermarket. It wrapped its lead round
peoples' legs. It wanted to fight dogs
and cats.

It tried to climb the steps of a fire-escape, and dragged Pat half-way up. It knocked over a box of apples. What a time Pat had getting that goat through the busy Pencaster streets! And when Sara saw it she nearly had a fit.

"What in the world are you doing with a goat?" she said.

"We've bought it," said Julian.

"*Bought it?*" said Sara.

"It was an accident," said Pat.

"An accident?" said Sara. "How can you . . . ?"

"He nodded," said Julian.

"Nodded?" said Sara.

"And waved?"

"No!" said Sara.

"He did," said Julian. "And the man thought . . ."

"Which man?" said Sara.

"The auctioneer-man . . ."

"Oh, yes . . ."

"He thought dad wanted to buy the goat.

He said it was a bargain," said Julian.
"And it is. Some of them were much
more . . ."

"Oh," said Sara, "were they? And how
much was this one? And what in the
world are we going to do with a goat?
And where are we going to keep it?"

"We could milk it," said Julian.
"Goat's milk. Delicious."

"I love goat's milk," said Sara.

"And we could keep it in the garden,"
said Pat.